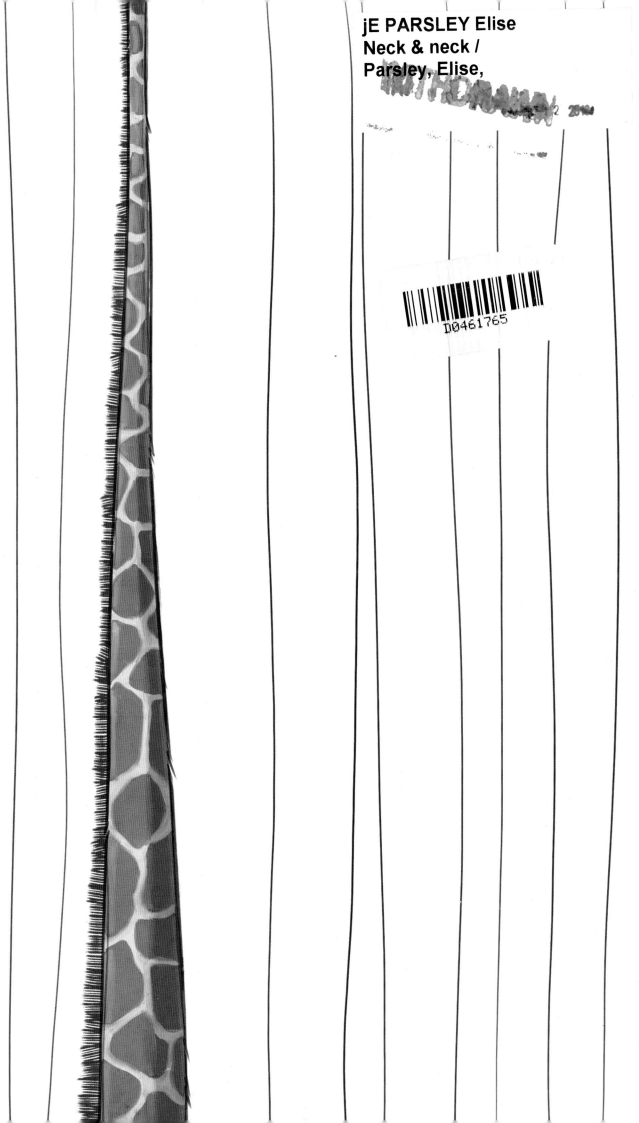

ELISE PARSLEY

NECK&
NECK

giraffe yums!

L B

Little, Brown and Company
New York Boston

Life at the zoo
was glorious for Leopold.
Every day, kids laughed and cheered,
and the snacks...
Oh, there were *such* delicious snacks!
This morning began with the usual
squeals of admiration.

*"Oh boy! Oh BOY!
The tallest animal
in the world!"*

*"I bet he can see all the
way to my house!"*

"I just love this guy!"

At that,
Leopold sighed and turned...

...and gasped

at the
gleaming smile

bobbing beside him.

"It's just like the real thing, only better," Leopold heard between giggles. "*This* giraffe is so cheerful!"

"Well, sheesh."

"*I* can be
cheerful too."
Leopold grinned.

"It zooms and
it bounces!"
said the kid.

"*I* zoom!
I bounce!"
thought Leopold.

"It's flexible!"
said the kid.

"It smells fresh."

"And I don't have to keep feeding *this* giraffe."

Leopold glanced at the snack dispenser. "Rats."

He huffed off to his favorite
tree for some alone time.

"*Well!* See if
I care about you
and that
grinning goofus!"

Up in the
prickly acacia tree,
Leopold sniffed
and sulked
and

—"OUCH!"—

was struck by an idea.

He chomped
off a branch.

Chaaaaaaaaaa

"And now that I have your
undivided attention,
bring on the laughter,
the cheers, and
a fistful of snacks!"

"Huh?"

Leopold pondered
where he had
gone wrong when—

The kid
hooted...

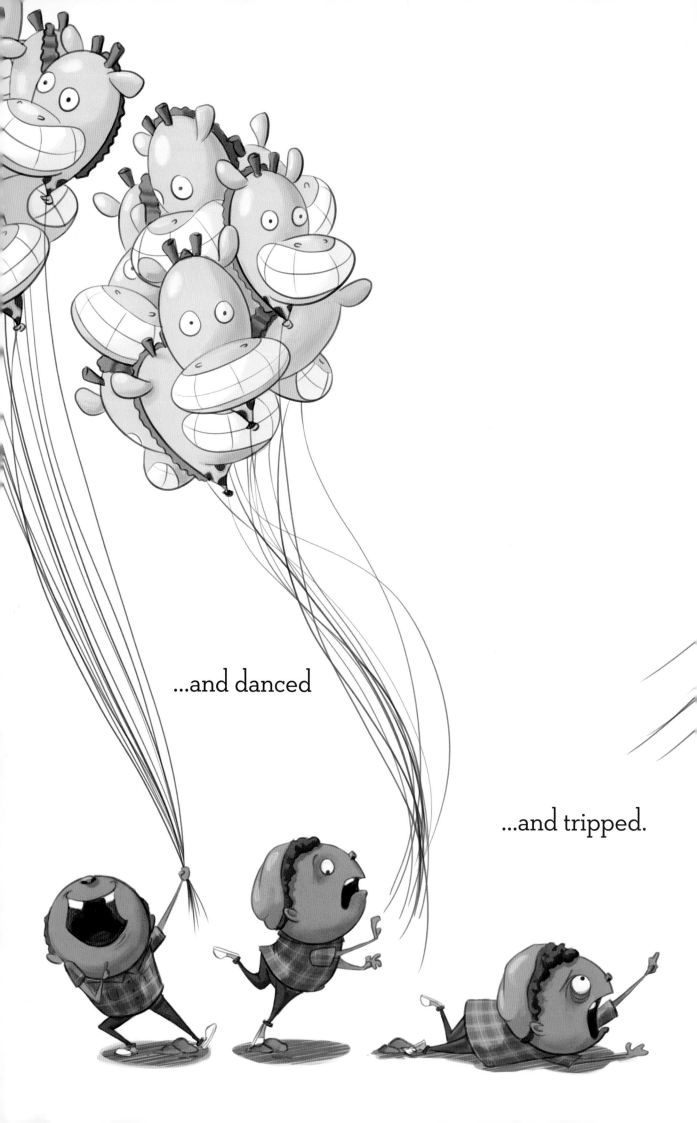

...and danced

...and tripped.

Leopold watched a dozen
scrawny necks drift up, up, up.

To save?

Not to save!

Leopold *alone* would be adored!

Right?

"Waaaahh!!"

Leopold stomped back to his tree.
"Honestly!
Those shiny airheads have
ruined everything.
Next thing you know,
they'll be taking over my habitat!"

Leopold groaned,

and sighed,

and stretched.

He cleared his throat.
"Fine, I give in.
I
just
can't
compete."

The kid jumped up.

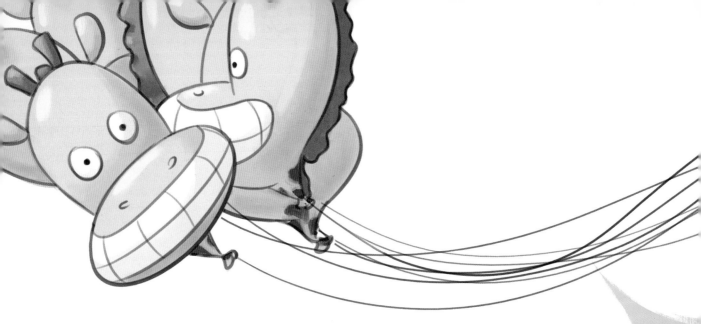

"You did it!"

he squealed.
"You saved them!
You used your
real, live, fuzzy, smelly,
looooong neck
and you saved them!"

There was laughter!

There was cheering!

And the snacks?

Those snacks tasted better than ever.

ABOUT THIS BOOK The illustrations for this book were digitally drawn in Adobe Photoshop and then painted in Corel Painter using a Monoprice tablet. This book was edited by Andrea Spooner and designed by David Caplan and Nicole Brown. The production was supervised by Erika Schwartz, and the production editor was Annie McDonnell. The text was set in Neutraface, and the display type is hand lettered.